Beware the Mare

BY JESSIE HAAS

Pictures by Martha Haas

A Beech Tree Paperback Book • New York

THANKS TO JOSEY,
WHO GAVE ME THE IDEA

1

"HERE HE COMES!" Lily calls from the kitchen window. She sees the old rattly truck turn into the driveway.

"About time!" Gran sniffs. She strikes a match

and lights the blue gas flame under the supper vegetables.

The truck's sides wobble, and the big springs creak. *Thud! Bang! Whinny!*

"There's a *horse* in the truck!" The door crashes. Lily is gone. Closing her lips firmly, Gran turns the vegetables off.

On the grassy bank in front of the old gray house, yellow daffodils bob. The air is filled with their perfume. It is very early spring. The trees are bare, but the fields are bright green, tempting the animals. Already the young steer has broken the fence three times.

Lily doesn't notice the daffodils or the green fields. She can think only of the truck and what might be inside it.

The truck stops, and Gramp hops down from the high seat. He wears green work clothes and a green cloth hat. Clamped in his teeth is a stained corncob pipe. Beneath the sign that says his name—LINWOOD GRIFFIN, LIVESTOCK DEALER—he stops to tap the pipe on his palm and put it in his shirt pocket. Gran has made him quit smoking, but Gramp still loves his pipe.

He looks up now and winks. "Lily, you're watching me just as sharp as your granny does," he says. "Don't you two trust a fellow?"

Gran thinks Gramp might still smoke his pipe sometimes when he's out alone in his truck. But Lily has seen that no ash came out when he tapped it. Gramp is only teasing. "I trust you," she says.

"That's good. Watch your toes, while I drop this tailgate."

Mom comes from the garden, where she has been digging. Her blonde hair is tied back under a red bandanna. From the house Gran walks out and stands with her arms folded across her apron front.

"What you got, Pop?" asks Mom.

"I *think* I got a deal," says Gramp, scratching his white bristles, "but I dunno."

He releases the stiff bolts at the back of the truck and lowers the heavy tailgate to the ground. Lily stands right behind it, so she can see as soon as the truck is open.

The truck is a dark cave, big enough to hold two workhorses. The bay mare in the cross-ties looks very small. She twists, looking over her shoulder at the big opening. The rims of her eyes show white. She whinnies loudly.

"Stand back, girls," says Gramp to all of them. He walks up beside the mare, speaking in a calm, clear voice.

"Easy there," he says. "Move over." He pushes with the flat of his hand, and the mare steps aside. Every move Gramp makes is slow and clear and easy to understand.

Now he unties her and leads her down the ramp. They both trot. She lands at the bottom and stops with her head high, looking toward the barn.

The other horses mill around, looking back and neighing: Stogie, the wild black Morgan; the Girls, who are workhorses; the three horses Gramp is going to sell; and the pony. The bay mare is bright-

eyed and eager to go meet them, but Gramp turns her away.

"Barbie," he says to Mom, "just lead her up and down the drive for me. I want to watch her move. Careful!" he warns as Mom takes the lead rope.

Gran looks at him sharply. "What's wrong with the animal?"

"Nothing, far as I can see." But if this is true, why does he sound puzzled, and why does he reach up under his green hat to scratch his head as he looks the mare over?

The mare is nervous. She holds her head high. Her little ears work back and forth, listening to the other horses and to the ping of the cooling truck hood. But she walks quietly beside Mom. She doesn't crowd; she doesn't shy; she doesn't try to nip.

"You want to trot her, Barb?"

"Why not?" says Mom.

"Careful," Gramp says again. What is he afraid of?

Mom runs down the driveway. The mare trots beside her. She is nervous, but she is trying very hard to be good.

"*Hmph,*" says Gramp. He sounds as if there is something he doesn't understand.

"She felt good to you?" he asks Mom.

"She's an angel!"

"*Hmph!*"

"She's pretty," says Lily, cautiously.

Usually when Gramp brings a horse home, he warns Lily, even before he lowers the tailgate: "Don't fall in love with this one. He's not a keeper."

Today he hasn't said that. This mare is just the right size for a girl outgrowing her first pony, the pony who was *Mom's* pony and is old and tired. What is wrong then? Why isn't the rope given to her? Why doesn't he say, "Here, Lily, she's yours?"

"She's sound, of course?" Mom says. Mom is wondering, too.

"Sound as a dollar—sounder! Feel those legs."

Mom runs her hand down all four legs.

"Perfect," she says. She stands back and looks.

The mare is shaggy. Her winter hair has shed out on her back and shoulders, but not yet on her belly. Her mane is tangled. She hasn't been brushed in a long time. But she looks strong and fine and lively.

Mom puts her arm around Lily's shoulders. "All right, Pop, what's wrong with her?"

"I . . . dunno," Gramp says. He looks embarrassed. "I don't like her name, that's all."

"You don't like her *name*?"

"Nope." He scratches under his green hat. "Ain't much to go on, is it?"

"What *is* her name?"

"Beware. Her name is Beware."

"Where did you buy this animal, Linwood?" Gran asks. Everyone else calls him Lin or Woodie. Only Gran calls him Linwood.

"I got her off Clyde Jones," Gramp says, and

Gran sniffs. Gramp and Clyde Jones are always trading horses, and one of them usually cheats.

"What did *he* say about her?"

Gramp glances at Lily. "I told him what I wanted her for. He said she's been a kid's horse. He's had her a couple months, out in the barnyard with the rest of 'em. No sign of trouble."

"Clyde wouldn't cheat you about something important," says Mom. *She* likes Clyde Jones.

"Course not," Gramp says, but he scratches under his hat again. He looks at Beware as if he is trying to see through her, see her bones, and see her past. "If it wasn't such a good deal, I wouldn't have thought twice. But I'm pattin' myself on the back, driving home, and it hit me. Beware. Beware of what?"

The mare pays no attention as her name is repeated. She is looking off at the other horses, with her ears forward and her eyes bright. She is beautiful. Lily's hand wants to close around the lead rope. . . .

"What did you pay for her?" Gran asks.

"Not a red cent," Gramp says. "Traded the steer for her."

Gran's face goes still. "That steer was meat for our table."

"The girl needs a horse, Gracie!" He turns away from Gran, taking the pipe out of his shirt pocket again. "I'll get another steer."

"There's six horses and a pony on this place right now!"

"Pony's too small." He isn't really listening. He clamps the pipe between his teeth, watching the mare thoughtfully. "Beware, huh? Well, I haven't seen you take one false step. Lily—"

"Linwood!" Gran's voice cracks like a whip. "Before you break that child's heart, and maybe her neck, you wait! You haven't owned this animal half an hour yet!"

Mom's hand tightens on Lily's shoulder, a quick little love squeeze.

"You find out who owned her before Clyde

Jones," says Gran, "and you make sure she's safe!"

Gramp reaches up and scratches under his hat. Gran watches sharply as the pipe turns upside down.

"All right," he says at last. "I don't know why they'd call you that, little mare, but just this once we'll listen to The Boss."

He turns to Lily. "Sweetheart, if she behaves herself, she's yours. But for now don't go near her unless I'm right there with you. Understand?"

Lily nods. She doesn't know if she should feel happy or not. "Can I pet her?"

"Yup. Move slow; you know how." He has taught Lily never to move quickly around horses. If you move quickly, they think there is something to fear. They may jump and hurt you, or they may kick.

"Hello," says Lily, softly but clearly. Horses like things to be clear. She puts her hand firmly on the mare's warm, smooth shoulder. "Hello, Beware."

2

EARLY THE NEXT morning, while the sky is still gray, Gramp comes to Lily's bedside.

"Wake up," he says, "and come on down to the barn."

Downstairs Gran is making coffee and sandwiches for Gramp's lunch. He's working on the road crew. Sometimes on Lily's way home from school she sees him out the bus window, leaning on the handle of a spade or raking hot black tar into a pothole.

"Linwood, what are you doing?" Gran asks as Gramp and Lily pass through the kitchen.

"We'll just get acquainted with the little mare," Gramp says. "And we'll load Mr. Steer in the truck," he tells Lily when the door has closed behind them.

Beware is in the barn, in a stall big enough for a workhorse. She looks very small in there. She has shavings in her mane.

"Good, she laid down to sleep," says Gramp. "That means she got to feeling calmer."

He goes to the wall and takes down a halter from a peg. He picks up a whip.

Lily watches. She knows Gramp would never

hurt a horse. He is always kind and fair. But she doesn't like to see the whip.

"Hey, Big Eyes!" He laughs at her. "Don't worry! This is just to make her turn and face me if she tries to kick."

"Will she?"

"Don't know. She must do something. You stand out here, Lily, and watch." He goes into the stall and pulls the door shut behind him.

Beware turns to look at him. She has been by herself all night. She is glad to see Gramp, even though he is not another horse. She takes two eager steps and reaches out her nose to him.

"Huh!" he says.

He leans the whip against the wall and puts the halter on Beware.

"All right, Lily, open the door."

Beware's eyes are bright. She steps eagerly to the door. But she is careful. Even though she is excited, she doesn't jump, and she doesn't push Gramp.

Gramp leads Beware to the cross-ties. He snaps

one rope in one side of her halter and the other rope in the other side. The two ropes hold her in the middle of the aisle.

"Stay back, Lily," Gramp says. "Maybe she won't stand tied." He walks away from Beware.

Beware watches him and bobs her nose. She would like to go with him. She hopes he won't leave her all alone.

But she stands still and waits.

"All right," says Gramp. "Maybe you bite." He walks back to Beware and holds out the flat of his hand. That is how you give something to a horse: make your hand like a table, and keep your fingers out of the way.

Beware drops her beautiful soft nose into Gramp's hand. She would like a treat, but he doesn't have one.

Gramp wiggles his fingers under her mouth. "Come on, little girl," he says, "try one! Look just like carrots, don't they?"

Beware gives a big, sad sigh and turns her head away.

"Well," says Gramp, "then maybe you kick." He walks all the way around Beware, very close to her. "This is the safe way, Lily," he says. "Stay close. If she does kick, she won't have room enough for a good swing. She'll only be able to push you."

Beware stands still.

"She's watching you," says Lily. Horses' eyes are different from people's. Horses can see behind themselves because their eyes are on the sides of their heads. Beware's eyes roll, following Gramp as he walks around her. Her ears follow him, too.

"Now I'll do it the wrong way," says Gramp. He walks quickly around Beware, close and then far. He walks straight up to her from behind, without speaking to her. He takes off his hat and flaps it. He holds the hat up in the air above Beware's head, and he passes it under her belly.

Beware stands still. One ear points one way, and

one points the other. She is confused, but she is trying to be good.

"So you don't kick," says Gramp. "Get me the brushes, Lily."

Lily brings him the round rubber currycomb and the hard brush and the soft brush. She sits on a hay bale and watches Gramp brush Beware. Beware's long winter hair falls onto the barn floor. Her coat is deep red, like a glowing coal. Her mane and tail and feet are gleaming black.

While Gramp grooms her, Beware stands still. Not once does she fidget or try to bite.

"I dunno," says Gramp, scratching under his green hat. "Nothing to beware of *yet*!"

Every morning for three days Gramp wakes Lily early. They go through the kitchen and stop on the front doorstep, to look around at the new day.

"Seen any blackflies yet?" Gramp asks Lily.

Every day Lily says, "Not yet."

Then they go down to the barn.

Every morning Gramp tries something different with Beware. And every morning he says, "You watch her for me, Lily." Gramp has taught Lily how horses speak. They hardly ever use their voices. They speak with their ears and with their faces. They speak in the way they move their bodies, the way they swish their tails, the way they stamp their feet.

"What's she saying?" Gramp asks as he stands in the corner of Beware's stall with his back turned.

Beware is coming up behind Gramp and poking his back with her nose. "She wonders what you're doing," Lily says. "She thinks you're crazy."

"And now what's she saying?" He is leading her down the driveway, the wrong way, walking in front with the lead rope loose and floppy.

"She wants to eat grass," says Lily.

"And now what's she saying?" Gramp is holding up one of Beware's back feet and trimming it with a hoof knife.

"She says she's bored," says Lily. "She wants to do something interesting."

Gramp straightens up and scratches his head. "Well, it beats me!" he says. He has called Clyde Jones, who can't remember the name of the people he bought Beware from and hasn't found the bill of sale yet. "Typical!" snorts Gran. Clyde Jones does remember that Beware was ridden by someone in Pony Club, and he knows what town she came from.

"If she went through Pony Club, she's had some good training," Gramp says. He's having Mom check with people she knew in Pony Club, to find someone who might remember Beware.

"But meantime, Lily, don't you go near her when I'm not around," he says.

But Gramp doesn't mean that Lily can't stand on a hay bale and look through the bars into the stall.

He doesn't mean that when Beware comes over and blows her sweet, hay-smelling breath on Lily's face, Lily has to back away. He doesn't mean Lily can't talk to Beware.

"You're not bad, are you, Beware? You're beautiful and good."

Beware pricks her ears to listen. Her eyes are soft and calm. Lily wants to pat her, but she knows she mustn't.

3

THE NEXT DAY when Gramp comes home, he has a saddle the right size for Beware. After he has groomed her and cleaned her feet, he puts the saddle on. He buckles the girth.

"Huh!" he says. "So you don't even bloat." Many horses take a big bellyful of air and hold it while the girth is tightened. When they let the air out, the girth feels loose and comfortable to them. But the saddle may slip, and the rider may get hurt.

"Get me that bridle on the wall," says Gramp. It is a bridle for a big horse. Beware is only a small horse. Gramp buckles every strap to the last hole. The loose ends of the straps hang long and flappy.

Beware makes bridling easy for Gramp. She lowers her head and reaches out for the bit.

Gramp scratches under his hat, tipping it so far back on his head that it almost falls off. "*No* deal is as good as this!" he says. "Lily, put on your hard hat and come out behind the barn, where your granny can't see us." He clips the long, white lunge line to Beware's bit and leads her outside. He carries the long whip.

Lily puts on the hard hat, which could save her life if Beware bucks her off. It feels as if something is jumping around inside her stomach. She is going to ride Beware.

But not yet. Beware has been in the barn a long time now. She is frisky and excited. Gramp lunges her.

He stands in one spot and makes Beware walk, trot, and canter around him in a big circle, at the end of the lunge line.

They are near the pasture. The Girls, Gramp's big chestnut work team, come to the fence to watch. That makes Beware want to show off. She kicks up her heels and races around the circle.

"Whoa!" Gramp says. Beware doesn't hear him. She is too excited and running too fast. Gramp pulls hard on the lunge line. "*Whoa!*" he shouts. Beware skids in a cloud of dust and faces him.

"Well!" he says. "That's better!" Is he pleased, Lily wonders, that Beware has finally done something bad?

"Now walk," he says.

Carefully Beware walks. She watches Gramp. She

doesn't want him to yell at her again. She walks when Gramp says "Walk," and trots when he says "Trot." Especially she whoas when he says "Whoa."

"Good girl," Gramp says, finally. "Now, Lily . . ." But his eyes never leave Beware. He sees her prick her ears and look toward the corner of the barn.

Cautiously Gramp turns his head, though he seems to keep one eye on Beware at the same time.

Mom comes around the corner of the barn. "What's up, Pop?"

"Don't you know better than to sneak up on a horse like that?" Gramp says.

"She knew I was coming," says Mom. "What's up?"

Gramp looks past Mom at the corner of the barn, but no one else is coming. "It's time to try her under saddle," he says.

"Are you going to ride her?"

"No, Barbie, I'm a fat old man, and I don't belong on a horse." He looks Mom over. She is young, for a mother, and light, and wearing blue jeans. *She* could ride Beware. . . .

No! Lily wants to cry. Let *me*! But she makes herself wait.

After a minute Gramp says, "All right, Lily. We'll hold her, and you can get on."

"Tighten your helmet strap, Lily," says Mom. She and Gramp stand on each side of Beware, holding the reins.

"I'll give you a leg up," says Gramp. "No sense pulling the saddle all around." He cups his free hand. Lily puts her knee into it, and Gramp boosts her up.

"Land light," he tells her. Lily is already settling herself softly into the saddle.

Beware looks around to see who is on her back. Her ears are pricked. Her eyes are soft and dark.

"Good mare," says Gramp. "Lily, gather up your reins so you can feel her mouth, and just hold them. I'll tell her what to do." He holds the lunge line and steps backward to the middle of the circle. "Walk."

Up till now Lily has done what Gramp told her. She hasn't fallen in love with Beware—at least, not more than she falls in love with every horse.

Now, as Beware walks, and trots, and then canters, Lily feels how wonderful everything could be.

The pony is old, and slow, and lazy, and stubborn. Lily loves him very much. But on Beware she could be free. She could do anything—jump logs on a trail, go for long canters, win ribbons at a horse show. Beware is listening to what Lily tells her. She hears the whispers of Lily's legs, so soft that even Gramp doesn't know about them. The pony is like a gruff old uncle, who doesn't want you to know he likes you. Beware wants to be a friend.

Now Gramp has Lily make turns and spirals and squiggles. He still holds the lunge line, but loosely. He just follows.

"Stop her," Gramp says. "Will she back?" She will.

"She hasn't put a foot wrong!" Gramp says to Mom. "I feel like a fool, Barbie! But since we started this, we'll keep going. Lil, time to hop off!"

Lily gets off, though she would rather not. "Take the saddle off," says Gramp.

Beware's back is sweaty under the saddle. Gramp has Lily brush her.

"Now," he says, "we'll turn her out with the other horses for a few days. Give her a pat, Lily, and thank her, because we won't touch her again for a while."

"Why not?" Gramp always knows best about horses, but Lily can't help asking.

"Sometimes when you turn them loose, they forget about people—like Stogie did. We want to find out if she's that kind."

"But if she is, couldn't we keep her where she won't forget about us?"

"If we had that kind of place, Lily. If we had

plenty of box stalls and board paddocks. But we just have an electric fence and big pastures. We need tame horses."

"Stogie isn't tame."

"And we don't need him. That's what your gran would say, and she's right."

4

WHEN LILY HAS thanked Beware and fed her a handful of grain, Mom leads the mare to the pasture gate.

By now all the horses have gathered. The Girls

tower over the rest, pointing friendly ears at Beware. The pony grazes at a distance. The three sale horses try to crowd closer, and Stogie chases them.

Since Gramp turned Stogie out in the big pasture two years ago, he has never once let anyone catch him. He bosses all the horses. Even the Girls get out of Stogie's way when he lays back his ears and takes his dangerous sideways step at them.

Gramp shakes his whip at the horses. "Go on, now!" he says. "Back up!"

The Girls move only a few steps. Stogie makes an evil face at Gramp. He takes a big prowling step at the other horses, telling them he is dangerous and that he will kick. They make mean faces, too, and flinch away and bite one another. Only the pony pays no attention.

"All right, Barbie," says Gramp. Lily opens the gate, and Mom leads Beware through. The horses all step toward her; Gramp raises his whip, and they stop. Mom takes off the bridle, and she and Gramp duck quickly under the fence.

The Girls want to sniff Beware. They look friendly. But Stogie takes a big, dangerous step at them and drives them back. He prances up to Beware, bending his neck in a high curve like a swan's neck. He and Beware sniff noses.

For a second they are very still. Lily can see their sides rise and fall. She can hear the big puffs of breath.

Suddenly there is an enormous squeal, like the sound an elephant would make. Stogie hits out at Beware with one front foot. Beware strikes, too. Then they arch their necks and sniff again.

"He'll *hurt* her!" cries Lily. There is another huge squeal.

"They didn't touch each other," Gramp says. He puts a hand on Lily's shoulder, and they stand watching.

Stogie and Beware squeal again. Then Stogie sees the other horses coming. They want to sniff Beware, too.

Stogie trots at them, going sideways and snaking

out his neck. They scatter. He bites one on the rump.

But the Girls sneak behind Stogie's back. Now they sniff Beware. All three noses are close together. All the ears point forward. All the necks arch.

This time the squeal sounds bigger than elephants—more like dinosaurs. Bess strikes. Her hoof is three times the size of Beware's.

Fiercely Stogie gallops back. He kicks Bess in the ribs with a solid thump. Babe and Beware tuck their tails and jump out of the way.

Now Beware is in the middle of all the other horses. Stogie can't keep them away. Beware is smaller than they are, and Lily can hardly see her in the crowd.

Stogie breaks through. He chases Beware, and all the other horses follow. Even the pony lifts his head for a moment. The whole herd thunders away, up the hill toward the woods. In a minute they are gone.

Lily feels herself starting to cry.

Gramp's hand tightens on Lily's shoulder. He gives her a little shake. "Don't worry," he says. "I never had one get hurt that way." He gives Lily his handkerchief. "Now you blow your nose and wipe your eyes, and maybe your granny won't ask us any questions."

After supper, when Lily goes out on the porch, she can see the horses grazing. They look small, like toy horses in the emerald pasture.

A black toy horse lifts its head. It sniffs noses with a toy horse the color of a glowing coal. There is a squeal. The tiny herd sweeps across the green pasture. Lily can barely hear the drumming of their hooves.

But in the morning Gramp wakes Lily early. "Look out your window," he says.

From her window Lily can see the pasture. She can see a little bay horse grazing. As she looks, another horse goes over. They arch their necks, sniff, and squeal softly, and then they go back to eating.

Beware stays loose in the big pasture for two days. Each morning before breakfast Gramp and Lily walk down to the barn together. Gramp looks at all the horses, to make sure they haven't hurt themselves. But he doesn't go into the pasture. "We have to give it an honest test, Lily," he says.

On the third morning, as Gramp and Lily go out onto the front step, the blackflies come. Blackflies are tiny flies that gather in clouds and bite. Gramp and Lily must put fly repellent on before they can go to the barn.

The blackflies bite the horses, too. They crawl inside ears, and they make tender bellies bumpy and itchy. Now Gramp must catch all the horses, every day, and put fly repellent on them.

The Girls stand patiently, with just a lead rope over their necks. They know Gramp is trying to help them. The sale horses try to be good, but Stogie chases them. He would like to chase Gramp, too. He makes an evil face and takes a dangerous, prowling step.

"Oh, no, you don't!" says Gramp, showing him the whip. Stogie tosses his head angrily and runs away. He stands under a tree, shaking his head and stamping his feet.

"I'm sorry for you," says Gramp, "but it's your own danged fault. If you ever see a horse coming at you like that," he tells Lily, "get out of the way!"

He puts fly repellent on the pony. Beware walks up behind him. When he turns around, she is standing there with her ears forward.

"Well, I guess you didn't go wild on us," Gramp says, scratching under his hat. "Lily, run get me a halter. We'll put her and the pony in the other pasture, and when I get home tonight, you can ride her again."

□ □ □

It is hard for Lily to wait all afternoon, from the time the school bus lets her off till the time when Gramp's truck rolls into the driveway. She walks down to the pastures. Beware and the pony doze in the shade. The Girls stand under a tree, scratching each other's shoulders with their whiskery upper lips. If one stops, the other nudges her and scratches harder, until both are at it again. Stogie, who feels very cross because of his bug bites, chases the sale horses around as they try to graze.

Lily scratches her own bug bites. She tries to think of something to do.

At last the truck rattles into the yard. Gramp stops to talk with Gran a minute. Lily can hardly stand the delay, but when she comes up, they are talking about Beware.

"Her name used to be Lady," Gramp is saying. "Barbie's friend told me that much."

"Lady's a nice normal name."

"If I had a dime for every mare I've owned named Lady," says Gramp, "I'd be a rich man!"

"*Hmph!*" says Gran. "If you'd *made* a dime on every horse you've owned, I could see some sense to it!" Pause. "Have you talked to the owners yet?"

"They're away," says Gramp. "Back next week. But Barbie's friend never heard anything bad about the mare. So—"

He pauses to take out his pipe. He is standing on the front step, and Gran is on the porch, with a panful of parsnips for supper. Gramp puts the pipe between his teeth, at a jaunty angle. He reaches back and cuffs his hat down over his eyes a little. "So, Gracie," he says again, "Lily's going to ride that horse, and if it goes all right, she'll keep her. She's waited long enough!"

Gran thins out her lips. She says, "You and I will never agree what's long enough, Linwood, but I'll say yes, if you'll agree to something."

"What is it?" Gramp asks. Beneath the hat and behind the pipe bowl, his face is mostly hidden.

This is how he looks when he's trading horses.

"I want you to agree, Linwood—and you, Lily—that if the horse proves dangerous, even later on, you'll let her go."

"Of course!" says Gramp. He sounds angry.

"There isn't any 'of course' about it, Linwood. That black devil is still out there, no use to anyone, and no chance of getting your money back—"

"Anytime you walk out there and catch him, Gracie, I'll sell him!" says Gramp. He shoves his pipe into his pocket. "Come on, Lily."

5

ALL THE WAY down Gramp's face looks hard and tight. But at the barn he suddenly says, "Well!" and squashes his hat back to its usual position. He winks at Lily. "Get the halter," he says, "and go on out and catch her."

Lily's heart beats hard as she ducks under the fence. "Be good," she whispers. "Please be good."

The pony looks up from his grass. He doesn't see a grain pail, and he goes back to eating.

Beware stands looking for a minute, with grass dribbling out of her mouth. Then she walks to meet Lily.

"Easy," Lily says. Beware puts her head down, and Lily slips the halter on.

"That was a pretty sight," says Gramp. He opens the gate for Lily. "Now lead her to the barn, and get her ready to ride. I want to see how you do it."

Gramp has taught Lily how to do everything. She knows how to curry a horse, moving the flat rubber currycomb in circles so the dirt and loose hair fall. She knows how to brush a horse smooth and slick with the soft brush. She knows how to clean a horse's hooves with the hoof-pick, and she knows to do this before every ride, in case the horse has a stone in its foot.

But she is used to doing it all for the pony, who is little and never puts himself to the trouble of taking an extra step. She is very careful with Beware.

Beware is careful, too. She stands still. Her eyes are bright and thoughtful.

"This mare loves to be fussed over," says Gramp.

Beware is much taller than the pony. Lily must reach way up to put the saddle on her back. She can't reach to bridle Beware at all. But before she has to ask Gramp, Beware gently lowers her head. She opens her mouth for the bit.

Gramp scratches under his hat. "I'm beginning to wonder if she might be a little *too* tame," he says. "You need a horse you can have fun on!"

But Gramp hasn't ridden Beware. He hasn't felt her quick, smooth step, or her understanding mouth, or her eagerness for a signal. Beware wants to have fun, whenever Lily is ready.

"Take her into the pasture," Gramp says, "and

ride her there. Do what you want to. I'll watch from the gate."

Now Lily is afraid. She would like to ride Beware where no one can watch. Then if either of them makes a mistake, no one will have to know.

"Be good," she whispers. "Be good." She stretches her foot way up to reach the stirrup, and grabs a handful of Beware's mane, and pulls herself into the saddle.

"Better use a mounting block next time," says Gramp. "Well, go on! Have fun!"

Now there is no lunge line on Beware. There is nothing to make her be good if she doesn't want to.

Very softly Lily squeezes with her legs.

Very slowly Beware walks.

They go past the pony. He doesn't lift his head. They go far out along the pasture fence, to where the land drops down. When Lily looks back, all she can see is hill. Gramp is out of sight.

Lily tightens the reins and speaks softly to Beware. "Trot!"

They are hidden, and they are free. When Lily tightens the reins and Beware stops too quickly and Lily almost falls off, no one sees. Lily can settle back into the saddle and get her balance and tell Beware to canter. No one is worried. They come to the brook that crosses the end of the pasture. Beware jumps it, and Lily almost falls off again. She turns Beware in a circle, and they jump the brook once more.

Again Lily's seat leaves the saddle. But this time she doesn't lurch. This time she floats free with Beware, light and easy over the brook. Beware keeps cantering, up the hill and back toward the gate.

Mom stands there beside Gramp, and Gran is coming down the hill. Gran never comes to the barn, but there she is, stepping disdainfully around the horse manure.

Lily slows Beware down. The trot is bumpy. She bounces around in the saddle, and she can't stop laughing.

"We jumped the brook!" she says. "Whoa!" Beware stops instantly. Lily is jolted forward onto Beware's neck. She hugs all of it that she can reach.

Gramp's grin can get no wider. He tears the green hat off his head and throws it on the ground and dances a couple of steps right on top of it. Then he puts it back on and turns to Gran.

"Well, Gracie? Well?"

Gran tries not to smile, but for once she can't help it. "Now I'll have to wash that hat, Linwood," she says, and turns away.

"Never gives an inch, Gracie," says Gramp proudly. "Well, it's official, Lily. She's yours, and this is your pasture. You keep the mare and the pony here and take care of them all by yourself. Think you can do that?"

"Of *course*!" says Lily.

Gramp slaps Beware on the neck. "Good little mare!" he says. "We'll find out about that name, for curiosity's sake, but I guess it won't mean much.

But, Lily, don't you get careless, even so. Don't take her out on the trail or the road till your mother can ride along with you."

"Oh, Pop—" Mom protests.

"Now, Barbie, I think it's only plain caution, don't you?" He cuffs his hat over his eyes and watches Mom from under the brim. He's always trying to get Mom to ride more.

"Yes, I suppose!" Mom knows exactly what he's up to, and she makes a face at him.

"I'll show you which one of the sale horses to use." But before Gramp turns away, he reaches up and shakes Lily's knee. "Go on," he says again. "Have fun!"

6

NO ONE NEEDS to tell Lily and Beware to have fun.

No longer does Lily have to kick a pony's fat sides, hard, when she wants to go faster. No longer does she have to pull hard on the reins to slow down. No longer must she pass by a little log to jump or a nice flat stretch for cantering.

Beware comes to the fence every time she sees Lily. As soon as the pony realizes that he won't be asked to work, he comes, too. The pony comes for treats. Beware comes because she wants to do something.

One day Mom rides out with them on one of the sale horses. They go up the trail to the woodlot. Beware steps eagerly and looks around at the new sights. But she doesn't shy, even when a partridge flies up beside her with a sound like a roll of drums.

After that Lily can go out alone. Beware likes that best. She walks along with her neck stretched and her ears pointed forward. When she comes to a bend in the trail, she steps more eagerly, looking ahead for the fresh view. If she sees a log, she wants to jump it. If she sees a deer running, she wants to follow it.

Every morning, before breakfast, Lily and Gramp go to the barn together. Gramp gets his big can of fly repellent and his rag. Lily gets her small can and *her* rag. They each go to their own pastures and put fly repellent on their own horses.

The fly repellent doesn't work perfectly. Some strong blackflies bite anyway. Lily does her best, but Beware still gets little bumps inside her ears and on her belly.

"That's not too bad," says Gramp when Lily calls him to look. "Better than poor old Stogie." Stogie stands under a tree with his ears flattened out to the sides. His ears are full of itchy, stinging bites.

"They're driving him crazy," says Gramp. "Wish I could convince him I want to help." He rubs the bumps on Beware's belly. Beware makes her upper lip long, the way the Girls do when they scratch each other's shoulders. She bends herself almost in a circle, and she scratches Gramp's arm with her lip.

"Itch, don't they?" says Gramp. "Never mind, blackfly season will be over soon. Then there's just deerflies and horseflies and botflies and face flies. . . . Makes you glad you aren't a horse, eh, Lily?" Then Gran rings the bell on the porch, and it is time for breakfast.

Today Gramp says, "I sold that sorrel to somebody over where your mare comes from, Lily. After I deliver him, I'll go see what I can find out."

Gramp isn't back when Lily gets home from school. She puts on her riding clothes and goes down to catch Beware.

The afternoon is warm and sunny, and the blackflies are hungry. Beware and the pony stand head to tail in the shade. They scratch each other's shoulders with their teeth. They butt their heads into each other's sides to rub the flies away. For the first time Beware does not come when Lily calls.

"I'll put some bug stuff on you," Lily promises. She ducks under the electric fence and walks across the pasture.

Suddenly Beware shakes herself hard, all over,

and comes trotting toward Lily. When she gets close, she slows down, but she puts her ears back. She comes at Lily with a prowling sideways step.

"If you ever see a horse come at you like that," Gramp has said, "get out of the way."

But now Lily is in the middle of the open pasture. There is nowhere to go. She is too surprised and too afraid to think. She only steps back one step. Beware follows with a big, dangerous stride. She flattens her ears. She pushes Lily with her belly. Lily steps back. Beware follows.

Now Lily can think. She can think what it will feel like to be kicked. She can think of what Gran said: "If the horse proves dangerous, you'll let her go."

"Oh, *Beware!*" she says. "Oh, *please* be good!"

Beware takes another sidestep. Look out! she is saying. Beware! I'm dangerous; you'd better do what I want! *Bump!*

Lily almost falls down. She should hit Beware with the halter. . . . *Bump!* Beware pushes with her belly. "Stay close," Gramp has said. "She'll only be able to push you." *Bump!* Lily's hands go out to keep herself from falling. She touches the bug bites on Beware's belly.

Beware stops moving. She lets out a huge sigh and turns to look at Lily. Her ears are forward now. She bends in a circle, as far as her neck will stretch. She nudges Lily's arm and scrubs with her upper lip.

Lily moves her hand. Beware's eyes brighten. She scrubs harder with her lip.

"*Oh!*" says Lily. Her heart is beating so hard she can barely breathe. Softly she scratches Beware's itchy bug bites.

Beware scratches back, just as she did with the pony a minute before and just as she did with Gramp this morning. She scratches in a bossy way. Harder! she tells Lily, with her firm, scratchy lip. If Lily stops, if she moves away, Beware puts back her ears and follows. She bumps Lily with her side. She pushes with her nose.

"Careful!" Lily says. She leans against Beware's side. She feels weak. She almost feels like crying. But she keeps scratching Beware's belly until her arm is tired.

"All right," she says. "That's enough."

I'm dangerous, Beware tells her. But Lily tells Beware right back: "Don't be a brat. I'll scratch you again later."

Beware sighs. She lets Lily put the halter on and follows to the gate. Her ears are forward now. She is ready to have fun.

Gramp comes home just at suppertime. He sails his green hat across the room to the top of the coat-rack, washes his hands, and sits down to the table. He takes a baked potato from the bowl. "Hot potato!" He tosses it from one hand to the other and winks at Lily. "Found something out, today!"

"Me, too," says Lily.

Even without his hat and pipe, Gramp gets his horse-trading look. "Did you find out the same thing I did, I wonder?"

Lily tries the horse-trading look herself. She makes her eyes narrow and holds her mouth still. "What did you find out?"

"All right, you two!" Mom says. "Is this about Beware?"

Gramp nods, and Lily nods. They don't look away from each other.

"Then *talk*!"

Lily keeps her eyes narrow. Gramp starts laughing. "You win!" he says. "They're nice people—glad the mare has a good home. And I found out about the name."

"*And?*" says Gran sharply.

"And the reason for the name," says Gramp, "is just this. . . ." Now he watches Lily carefully. He springs his words on her one by one, trying to guess how much she knows. "In blackfly season—when her belly gets itchy—this mare likes—"

"To have it scratched!" shouts Lily.

"That's right," says Gramp. "Scare you?"

Lily nods.

"But you figured it out."

"Yes."

"Why *should* she be scared?" Gran asks. "Linwood?"

Gramp takes time to butter his potato before he answers. "Well, Gracie, did you ever stop to think about how a horse tells another horse to do something?"

"I never think about horses at all if I can help it!"

"They're more interesting than you might guess," says Gramp. "They never say please, for one thing. If they want a nice scratch, they come up to another horse—or to you—and start in scratching."

"Go on," says Gran grimly.

"So come blackfly season, this mare learned it felt good to have her belly curried. And if it feels good then, why not anytime? So one day the girl that owned her is out in the pasture when up comes Lady with her ears back—"

"Just like Stogie," says Lily. "Like she's going to kick."

"And does she?" Gran asks—not of Lily but of Gramp.

"No," says Gramp. "She won't do any more than bump you with her belly. But it's scary. They came close to selling her before the girl figured it out." Gramp winks at Lily. Lily knows he is proud because *she* figured it out right away.

"So her name *was* Lady," Mom says.

"I was brought up to think it was bad luck," says Gran, "changing an animal's name."

"Me, too," says Gramp, "but they weren't. Started as a joke—better beware the mare, and so forth—and then it got to be a nickname, and pretty soon they started putting it down on entry forms for shows. Sounded more exciting, I guess."

Mom and Lily meet each other's eyes.

"Anyway, Gracie," says Gramp, "you were right

to have me be careful. She's a good little horse, and now we know. What you going to call her, Lil? Lady?"

"Her name is Beware," says Lily. She has finished her supper, and she gets up from the table.

"Where are you going?" asks Mom.

"Down to say good-night."

"Don't get knocked down!" Gran warns. Gramp winks at Lily, and Mom smiles down at her plate.

Lily walks down the path to the pasture. It is cool out and almost completely dark. The flies have gone away. She can smell the daffodils and hear the peepers in the pond.

When she reaches the pasture gate, Beware and the pony are nowhere in sight. Lily ducks under the electric fence. "Beware!" she calls. "Beware!" She hears a nicker and the soft thud of hooves, and then Beware is there. Lily holds out her hand. Beware drops her velvety nose into Lily's palm for a moment. Then she swings her belly around. *Bump!*

"Yes, Beware," says Lily. She leans against Beware's warm, sleek, horse-smelling side. She reaches under Beware's belly, and she scratches.

Beware sighs deeply. She braces her legs, and cranes her neck all the way around, and scratches back. The big warm curve she makes around Lily feels almost like a hug.